Henny-Penny

A Puffin Easy-to-Read Classic

retold by Harriet Ziefert
illustrated by Emily Bolam

PUFFIN BOOKS

PUFFIN BOOKS
Published by the Penguin Group
Penguin Putnam Books for Young Readers,
345 Hudson Street, New York, New York 10014, U.S.A.
Penguin Books Ltd, 80 Strand, London WC2R ORL, England
Penguin Books Australia Ltd, 250 Camberwell Road, Camberwell, Victoria 3124, Australia
Penguin Books Canada Ltd, 20 Alcorn Avenue, Toronto, Ontario, Canada M4V 3B2
Penguin Books (N.Z.) Ltd, 282-290 Wairau Road, Auckland 20, New Zealand

Penguin Books Ltd, Registered Offices: Harmondsworth, Middlesex, England

First published in the United States of America by Viking,
a division of Penguin Books USA Inc., 1997
Published simultaneously by Puffin Books,
a division of Penguin Putnam Books for Young Readers, 1997

11 13 15 17 19 20 18 16 14 12

Text copyright © Harriet Ziefert, 1997
Illustrations copyright © Emily Bolam, 1997
All rights reserved

Puffin Easy-to-Read ISBN 0-14-038188-0

Printed in the United States of America
Set in Bookman
Puffin® and Easy-to-Read® are registered trademarks of Penguin Putnam Inc.

Reading Level 1.6

Henny-Penny

One day Henny-Penny
went for a walk.
An acorn fell.

The acorn hit Henny-Penny
on the head!

"Oh, dear," said Henny-Penny.
"The sky is falling.
   I must go and tell the king."

On her way she met Cocky-Locky.

"Where are you going?"
asked Cocky-Locky.

"I am going to tell the king
the sky is falling,"
said Henny-Penny.

"I'll come with you,"
said Cocky-Locky.

On the way they met Ducky-Lucky.
"Where are you going?"
asked Ducky-Lucky.

"We are going to tell the king
the sky is falling," they said.

"I'll come with you," said Ducky-Lucky.

On the way they met Goosey-Loosey

"Where are you going?"
asked Goosey-Loosey.

"We are going to tell the king
the sky is falling," they said.

"I'll come with you,"
said Goosey-Loosey.

On the way they met Turkey-Lurkey.
"Where are you going?"
asked Turkey-Lurkey.

"We are going to tell the king
the sky is falling," they said.
"I'll come with you,"
said Turkey-Lurkey.

Then they met Foxy-Loxy.
"Where are you going?"
asked Foxy-Loxy.

"We are going to tell the king
the sky is falling," they said.

"You are not going the right way,"
said Foxy-Loxy. "I will show you
a good way to go."

So they followed Foxy-Loxy.

He stopped in front of a dark hole.
"This is a good way to go to the
king," said Foxy-Loxy.

Foxy-Loxy went in first.
Turkey-Lurkey followed him.

Goosey-Loosey went in next.

Ducky-Lucky followed Goosey-Loosey.

Cocky-Locky went in last.
Henny-Penny heard him cry,
"Run away, Henny-Penny!"

doodle doo!

Henny-Penny started to run.
She ran and ran . . .

. . . and ran!

She ran all the way home.
And she never told the king
the sky was falling!

5901